LITTLE LIBRARY

The Ugly Duckling

AND OTHER STORIES

Retold by Margaret Carter
Illustrated by Hilda Offen

Kingfisher Books

Kingfisher Books, Grisewood & Dempsey Ltd,
Elsley House, 24–30 Great Titchfield Street,
London W1P 7AD

First published by Kingfisher Books in 1993
2 4 6 8 10 9 7 5 3 1

BRITISH LIBRARY CATALOGUING IN PUBLICATION DATA
A catalogue record for this book is available from
the British Library
ISBN 1 85697 077 9

Designed by The Pinpoint Design Company
Phototypeset by Waveney Typesetters, Norwich
Printed in Great Britain by
BPCC Paulton Books Limited

Contents

The Ugly Duckling 9

The Rats' Daughter 14

The Little Red Hen and the Fox 20

Anansi and Common Sense 26

The Ugly Duckling

Hans Christian Andersen

Among the reeds, down by the river, a mother duck sat on her nest. The sun warmed her feathers, the reeds sang a rustling song and she was happy. And when her little ducklings came from their shells she was even happier.

She stroked them with her bill, she quacked a welcome, then she noticed something: one egg hadn't hatched.

She looked at the egg: it didn't look like one of her eggs. "Oh well," she thought and sat down again. And soon out came the last duckling.

Only he looked a bit odd – not so much odd as different. But she gave him a welcome, stroked his feathers and waddle, waddle, waddle, she led them all out for a swim in the river.

"What lovely babies," said all her friends. Then they looked at the last one. "He'll improve," said his mother. "Give him time, he'll improve!"

Only he didn't: he got worse. He was lumpy and clumsy and rather fat.

"I'll live by myself," he grumbled. Off he went and settled himself on the banks of a great marsh. Then one day he heard a strange cry and in the sky above him he saw three white birds. "How lovely they are," he said.

And he wished he could be just like them.

When spring came, the duckling grew restless. He flapped his wings and suddenly he was in the air and flying! He looked down to the water below and saw his reflection. He was a swan – a white swan!

"I wasn't a duckling," he said. "All the time I was a swan!"

And with joy in his heart he flew on in the clear spring sky.

THE UGLY DUCKLING

The Rats' Daughter

Traditional Eastern

Mr and Mrs Rat had a most lovely daughter. Her tail was long, her coat shone, her teeth were white – my, she was an elegant creature.

"She must marry the most powerful thing in the world," said Mrs Rat. "She must marry the Sun."

So they put the idea to the Sun who was polite but not interested.

"Thank you kindly," he said, "but the Cloud is more powerful than I am. When he floats in front of me no one can see my light nor feel my heat. Why not ask the Cloud?"

The Cloud was astonished at the idea. "Thank you for the offer," he said, "but the Wind is far more powerful than I am. Why, he can blow me right across the sky! He would make a splendid match for your daughter. Why not ask the Wind?"

So Mr and Mrs Rat went to ask the Wind.

The Wind wasn't at all keen. "But the Wall is more powerful than I am," he said. "However much I blow I cannot blow the Wall down. Why not ask the Wall?"

So Mr and Mrs Rat went to find the Wall.

The Wall looked down from a great height. "How kind of you," he began... But just then there was a noise.

It was the Rats' daughter.

She stamped her foot, she shook her paws, she screamed. "I don't want to marry a Wall," she yelled. "Nor a Sun, nor a Cloud, nor a Wind..."

"I was about to suggest," said the Wall smoothly, "that there is one far more powerful than I am."

"Who's that?" asked Mr Rat.

"A Rat," said the Wall. "If a Rat should nibble at my feet, then I would come tumbling down. Why not ask a Rat?"

And the Rats' daughter smiled.

So they asked a Rat, who was quite delighted. He was handsome, bold, a good match for her elegant looks. Now they were all happy – Sun, Cloud, Wind, Wall, but especially the Rats' daughter.

The Little Red Hen and the Fox

Traditional Irish and American

A little red hen lived alone in a house in the forest. She was a very tidy creature, always dusting, and in her pocket she kept a needle, thread and some scissors.

"Just in case," she would say.

Now the hen had an enemy: a fox. "That hen would make a fine supper," he'd think, but the hen took great care not to let him get too close.

Every time she went out she locked the door and took the key with her.

Until one day she forgot.

Whoosh! in went the fox and then when she came back, "Good-day, ma'am!" said he, smiling and showing all his great terrible teeth.

"Squawk!"
said the red hen
and flew up to the
rafters, losing quite a
few feathers on the way.

"Bother," said the fox. "I know
– I'll run round in circles so she won't
know where I begin and where I end.
Then she'll get dizzy and fall off her
perch."

Which she did. Thud!

"Hen for supper tonight," said
the fox, popping her into his sack.

And off he strode, whistling.

Hen sat very still until she heard Fox say, "Phew! This sack is heavy. I must have a rest!"

When she heard a snore, she took out her scissors and cut a hole in the sack. Out she wriggled and put a big stone inside in her place. Then she stitched up the hole and flew away.

When Fox woke up he picked up the sack and marched home. "Are you ready for supper, mother?" he called.

"All ready, my son," came the reply. "The table's laid, so into the pot with her!"

Fox opened the sack and splosh! in went the big stone. "You foolish boy!" screamed Mrs Fox and gave him a wallop with her ladle.

There was no supper for Fox that night. But in her cosy home Hen had a good meal and went to bed happy.

"You never know," she said, "when a needle, some thread and scissors will come in handy!"

And in the darkness the little red hen laughed and laughed.

Anansi and Common Sense

Traditional African and Caribbean

Anansi is a spider, big and black. He lives in a land where the sky is blue and the sun always shines.

One day, not having much to do, he packed all the common sense in the world into a calabash which is a sort of bag made out of a big fruit.

"Now I'll be cleverer than anyone else," he said, very pleased.

"I'll hide my common sense at

the top of a tree," he thought. So he tied a rope round the calabash and began to haul it up. My, it was heavy! He panted and he puffed.

"It's easier to carry it on your back," called a voice. "That's only common sense!" And there was a small boy, laughing at him.

Anansi was furious. How dare this boy still have common sense when he'd thought he'd collected it all?

In a great rage he threw down the calabash which at once split open. Out flew bits of common sense, all over the world – which is why we all have a bit. Only some of us have a lot more than others!

LITTLE LIBRARY

Red Books to collect:

Beauty and the Beast
and Other Stories

▲

Cinderella
and Other Stories

▲

Goldilocks
and Other Stories

▲

Little Red Riding Hood
and Other Stories